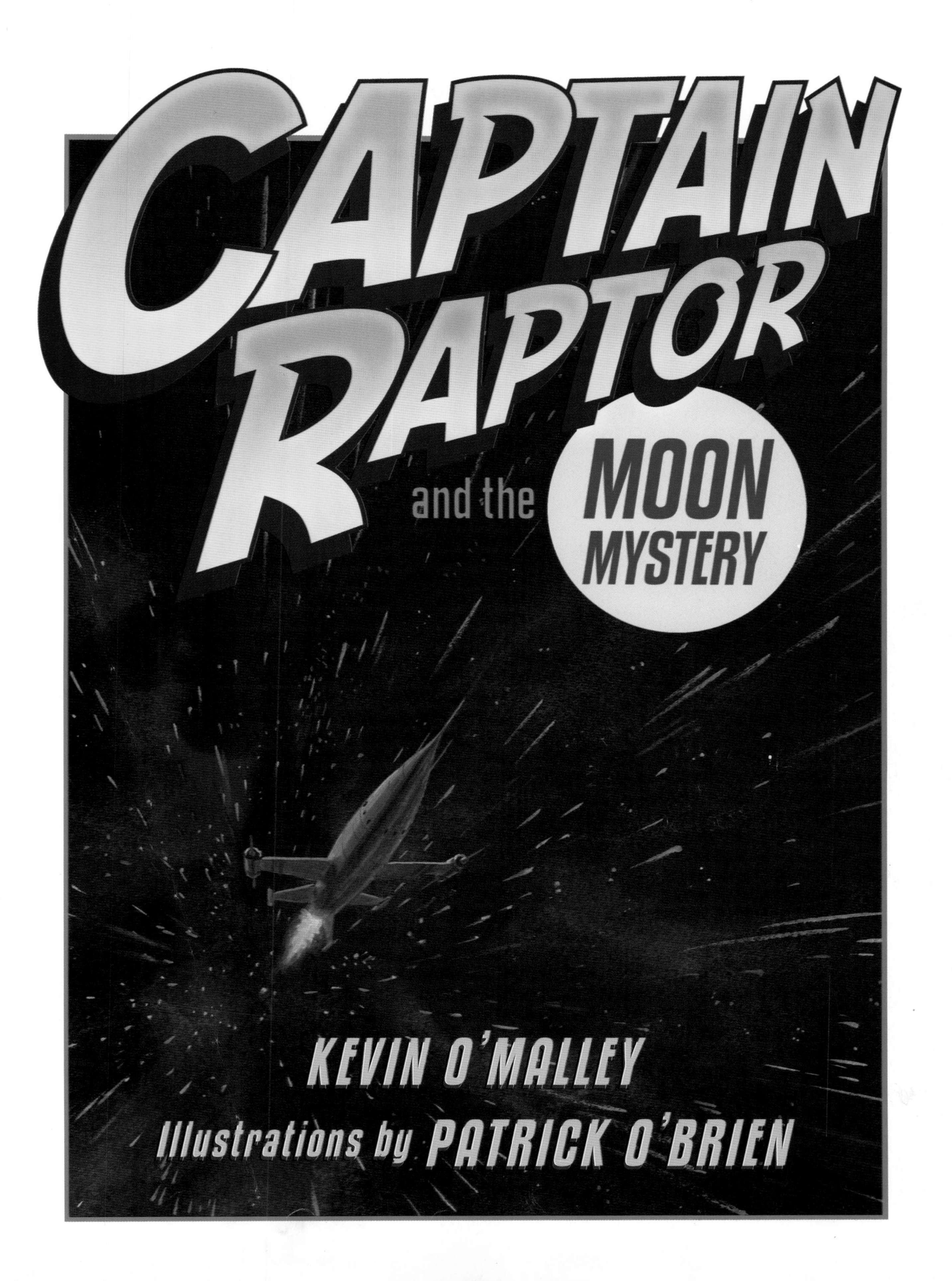
CAPTAIN RAPTOR
and the MOON MYSTERY
KEVIN O'MALLEY
Illustrations by PATRICK O'BRIEN

HIGH ABOVE THE PLANET JURASSICA, A ***FLASH OF LIGHT*** RACES ACROSS THE SKY AND DISAPPEARS ON THE DARK SIDE OF ***EON,*** THE PLANET'S MOST ***MYSTERIOUS*** MOON.

THE SCIENTISTS SAY THAT THEY MUST *INVESTIGATE.*

THE GENERALS SAY THAT THEY MUST *PREPARE FOR AN INVASION.*

THE PRESIDENT OF JURASSICA SAYS THEY MUST CALL . . .

CAPTAIN RAPTOR!

THE USD *MEGATOOTH,* CAPTAIN RAPTOR'S MASSIVE SPACESHIP, IS PREPARED FOR TAKEOFF.

"***SADDLE UP,*** FOLKS. NO TIME FOR TALKIN'. SOMETHING'S HAPPENING UP ON EON. ***WE'VE GOT A JOB TO DO!***"

CAPTAIN RAPTOR SETS THE ROCKET'S PLASMOCONTROLS FOR ***BLASTOFF***. WITH A TREMENDOUS ROAR THE MIGHTY *MEGATOOTH* LIFTS OFF AND ***RACES*** UP THROUGH THE CLOUDS OF JURASSICA.

"WITHIN THE HOUR WE WILL BE LANDING ON THE SURFACE OF EON. I DON'T WANT ANY SURPRISES, SO ***LET'S BE READY*** FOR ANYTHING."

SLOWLY THE *MEGATOOTH* DESCENDS THROUGH THE ELECTRICALLY CHARGED ATMOSPHERE OF THE MOON OF EON. ***THUNDER CRASHES*** AND JAGGED BOLTS OF ***LIGHTNING*** CROSS THE SKY.

"***EVERYONE TO THEIR STATIONS AND BUCKLE UP!***" ORDERS CAPTAIN RAPTOR. "I'M LOSING CONTROL OF THE FORWARD ENGINES. REVERSE ENGINES ARE OFF-LINE. HOLD ON TIGHT FOLKS—***WE'RE GOING IN THE HARD WAY!***"

THE MIGHTY *MEGATOOTH* **SLAMS** INTO THE RAGING SEA . . . AND IS TOSSED ABOUT LIKE A TOY.

"WE CAN'T TAKE TOO MUCH MORE OF THIS POUNDING!" SHOUTS CAPTAIN RAPTOR. "CONVERT THE SHIP TO UNDERSEA MODE. ON MY ORDER . . .
. . . ***DIVE, DIVE, DIVE!"***

WITH THE ENGINES DAMAGED, THE *MEGATOOTH* SINKS QUIETLY TOWARD THE BOTTOM OF THE DARK SEAS OF EON.

"PROFESSOR, I NEED YOU TO GET THOSE ENGINES BACK UP AND RUNNING!"

"I'M WORKING AS FAST AS I CAN, CAPTAIN. GIVE ME A FEW MORE MINUTES!"

"CAPTAIN, I'M DETECTING A STRANGE ENERGY SIGNAL FROM AN OBJECT ON THE SEAFLOOR. IT'S LIKE NOTHING I'VE EVER SEEN."
"OKAY THREETOE, WE'LL TAKE A LOOK AT IT WHEN WE GET MOVING."

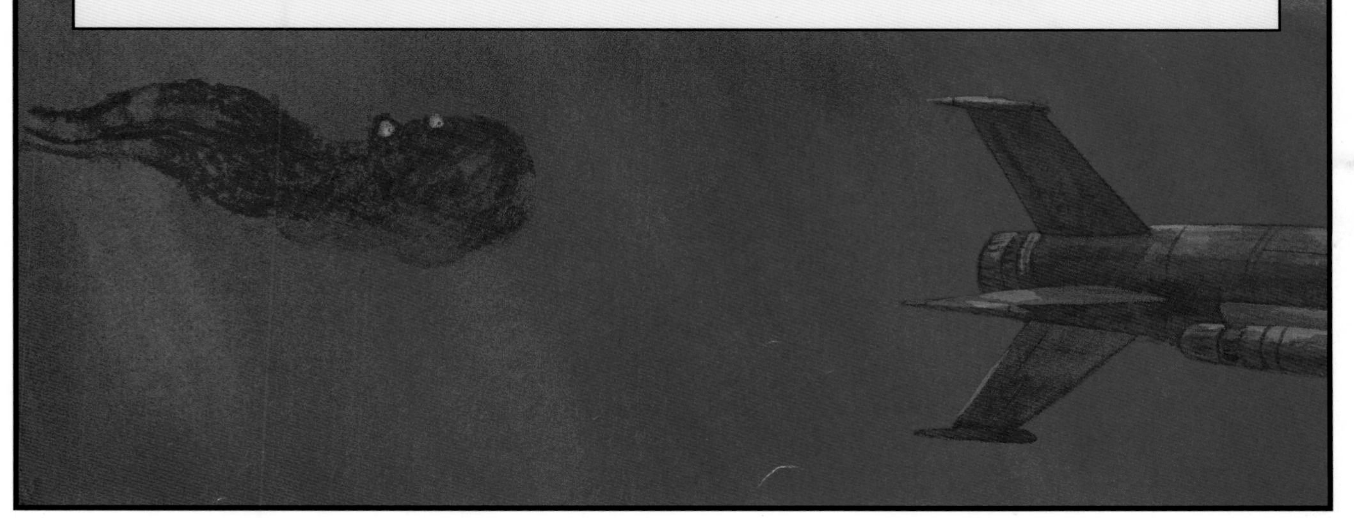
LITTLE DOES THE FEARLESS CREW SUSPECT THE HORRIFYING SURPRISE THAT CREEPS THROUGH THE INKY DEPTHS TOWARD THE SHIP.

OctoColossus!

The dreaded beast of the Sea of Eon slowly wraps its ***giant tentacles*** around the *Megatooth.*

"CAPTAIN, ***THE SHIP CAN'T TAKE THE PRESSURE.*** THE MONSTER IS ***SQUEEZING US*** LIKE A TUBE OF TOOTHPASTE!"

COULD **THIS** *BE THE END OF CAPTAIN RAPTOR AND HIS FEARLESS CREW?*

"SETTLE DOWN EVERYONE. PROFESSOR, RIG UP AN ELECTROPHOTONIC PULSE AND RUN IT THROUGH THE HULL OF THE SHIP. LET'S GIVE OLD OCTY ***A LESSON IN MANNERS.***"

THE ***SHOCK*** IS TOO MUCH FOR THE BEAST. OCTOCOLOSSUS RELEASES ITS GRIP AND SLINKS AWAY.

"NEXT TIME ***KEEP YOUR SUCKERS TO YOURSELF.***"

"OKAY CREW, LET'S NOT WAIT AROUND TO SEE IF THE BEAST COMES BACK. THREETOE, WE'RE GOING TO CHECK OUT THAT STRANGE ENERGY SOURCE YOU FOUND DOWN THERE."

THE *MEGATOOTH* RELEASES THE MINISUB AND PROFESSOR ANGLEOPTOROUS MANEUVERS IT SLOWLY TO THE SEAFLOOR.

"FASCINATING," SAYS ANGLEOPTEROUS. "IT APPEARS TO BE SOME SORT OF ENGINE."

GINGERLY HE NUDGES THE OBJECT WITH THE MINISUB'S ROBOT ARMS, THEN PICKS IT UP AND CARRIES IT BACK TO THE *MEGATOOTH*.

WITH THE REPAIRS COMPLETED, THE *MEGATOOTH* FINALLY SURFACES IN A QUIET INLET.

OVER THE RIVER OF HYDROPHILLUS AND AROUND THE CLIFFS OF ACROPHOBIUS, THE CREW OF THE *MEGATOOTH* MARCH DEEP INTO THE ***UNKNOWN WILDERNESS*** OF EON.

FROM THE CREST OF A ROCKY RIDGE, THE CREW SPOT SOMETHING ***STRANGE*** IN THE VALLEY BELOW. THREETOE RAISES HIS MAGNIVIEWER FOR A CLOSER LOOK.

"***IT'S A SPACESHIP,***" HE SAYS, "AND IT LOOKS LIKE IT CRASH-LANDED. ***WAIT A MINUTE***—THERE ARE SOME KIND OF ***WEIRD CREATURES*** DOWN THERE! THEY HAVE NO SCALES, NO HORNS, AND THEY DON'T EVEN HAVE ***TAILS!***"

"FASCINATING," SAYS THE PROFESSOR.

CAPTAIN RAPTOR TAKES THE MAGNIVIEWER AND PEERS SILENTLY AT THE ALIENS. SUDDENLY HE STANDS UP AND STARTS DOWN THE STEEP SLOPE.

"LET'S FIND OUT WHO, OR WHAT, HAS DROPPED IN. BUT BE CAREFUL. I DON'T LIKE THE LOOKS OF THEM, THEY COULD BE DANGEROUS."

CAPTAIN RAPTOR AND HIS CREW PUSH THROUGH THE DARK AND TANGLED JUNGLE, THEN STEP SUDDENLY INTO A CLEARING. THE ALIENS ARE STARTLED. SOME REACH FOR THEIR WEAPONS, WHILE OTHERS STARE IN SHOCK. NO ONE DARES MOVE.

THE JUNGLE HEAT BEGINS TO FEEL LIKE AN INFERNO. SWEAT RUNS DOWN THE ALIENS' SMOOTH SKIN.